MARVEL

A BLACK PANTHER GRAPHIC NOVEL

INTO THE HEARTLANDS

WRITTEN BY
ROSEANNE A. BROWN

ILLUSTRATED BY
DIKA ARAÚJO, NATACHA BUSTOS & CLAUDIA AGUIRRE

LAYOUTS 91-104 BY
GEOFFO

COLORS BY
CRIS PETER

LETTERS BY
VC's ARIANA MAHER

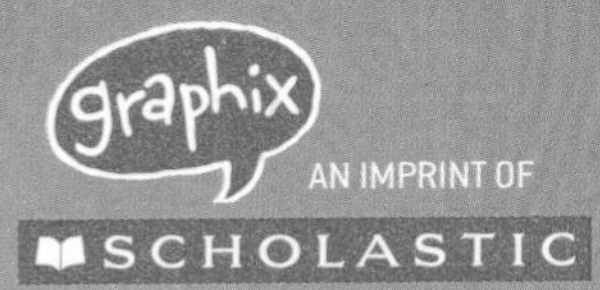

LAUREN BISOM, Senior Editor
CAITLIN O'CONNELL, Associate Editor
STACIE ZUCKER, Publication Design
JENNIFER GRÜNWALD, Senior Editor, Special Projects
SVEN LARSEN, VP Licensed Publishing
JEFF YOUNGQUIST, VP Production & Special Projects
DAVID GABRIEL, SVP Print, Sales & Marketing
C.B. CEBULSKI, Editor in Chief

Special Thanks to **WIL MOSS** and **DAN EDINGTON**

MICHAEL PETRANEK, Executive Editor, Manager AFK & Graphix Media, Scholastic
JESSICA MELTZER, Senior Designer, Scholastic

Black Panther created by **STAN LEE & JACK KIRBY**

Art by Dika Araújo, Natacha Bustos, and Claudia Aguirre
Cover art by Natacha Bustos and Cris Peter
Letters by VC's Ariana Maher

ISBN 978-1-338-64805-8

10 9 8 7 6 5 4 3 2 1   22 23 24 25 26

Printed in the U.S.A.   40

First edition, April 2022

CHAPTER ONE

I've never understood people who go to bed early.

I mean, all the best things happen at night.

Sleepovers...

...shooting stars...

...scientific breakthroughs.
It's alive!
IT'S ALIIIIIIIIIIIIVE!
The Wolf Diaries
That's me, Shuri. Princess. Intern at the Wakanda Design Group. Future world record holder for "Most Scientific Achievements on One Wikipedia Page Ever."
Someone has been working on her maniacal laugh.
All the best scientists have one.
K'Nemi. Fellow intern at the WDG. Super cool, but her style could use some work.
Okay, Dr. Frankenstein, your machine turns on. But does it actually work?
Allow me to demonstrate.

BEEP!
WHIR
WHIR
WHIR
Okay, that is pretty cool.
The board will have to make me a project lead when they see this!
TYME
Just imagine the possibilities! With enough of these bad boys, we could get rid of drought forever! End famine! Or... or...go sledding right here in Wakanda!
As much as I love the idea of sledding in East Africa in August, the board will never agree.

PFFFT
They've never picked a first-year intern as a lead. They might make an exception for the princess, but I've been here almost **three** years and I've **never** been picked.
Who cares about seniority? The best people should be the leads, and you and I are the best.
The old dudes who run the Design Group don't like change, and that's the way it's always been done.
That's ridiculous! The whole point of science is doing things that have never been done!
Things are going to change around here when I'm in charge. First order of business: rainbow lab coats for everyone.
I'm all for that plan, but shouldn't you get to bed? Tomorrow's a big day.
Ugh, don't tell me you're also obsessed with all this Soul Washing stuff.
We have, like, a million festivals a year. What makes this one so special?
The Soul Washing is the only ceremony that could get us all cursed by the ancestors if it goes wrong.
BASHENGA: A HISTORY
The Heartlands: FACT or MYTH
VIBRANIUM CORRUPTION
Pfft, right. Curses. Because those totally exist.
Says the girl whose family gets cat super-powers from a magic plant.
Touché.

Maybe I'd care more if my family would actually let me do something!
They wouldn't even let me help plan our gift to the ancestors! They were all like, "You'll get your turn when you're ready."

But you know who gets to talk tomorrow even though he STINKS at public speaking? T'Challa! It's so unfair!

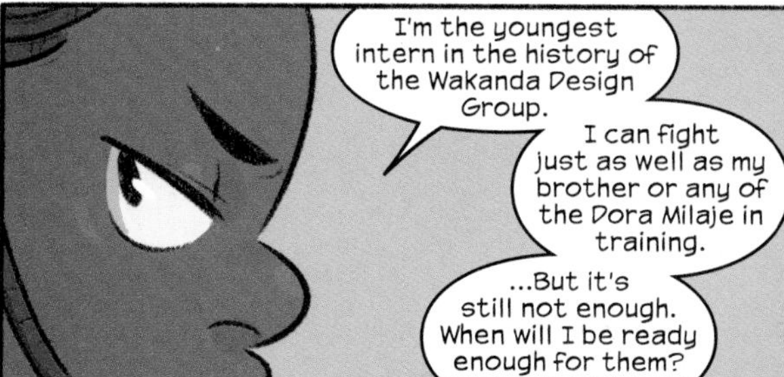
I'm the youngest intern in the history of the Wakanda Design Group.
I can fight just as well as my brother or any of the Dora Milaje in training.
...But it's still not enough. When will I be ready enough for them?

"I'm T'Challa and they let me give speeches just because I'm old enough to shave now!"
Ha!
"I'm so awesome! I'm so cool! Even though I can't talk to a girl without breaking out in hives and my room smells like sweaty gym socks and—"

So you admit you've been sneaking into my room?

Oh, you are in so much trouble.
T'Challa. Prince of Wakanda. Current holder of the "World's Most Annoying Human Being" award...and my older brother. (Unfortunately.)

BANG
MOM!

I found her playing in her lab even though you clearly said—
I wasn't *playing*, I had a breakthrough—
—never listens to anyone, should have been asleep hours ago—
—most important hing ever, could end global warming—
smelled like sweaty gym socks—
hy should punished for elling the truth. Ugh, you're such a snitch!
Well, you're a loudmouth!
You're short!
You're a stick-in-the-mud!
YOU TAKE THAT BACK, YOU—
Enough, you two.

I love you both very much.
But if you do not stop screaming in the next ten seconds...
...I will tie steaks to both your necks and leave you to fend for yourselves in the panther enclosure.
My mom, Queen Ramonda. People who think the Black Panther is the scariest person in Wakanda have never met her.

EEEEEEEEEEP

Bedtime exists for a reason. Even if you're not tired, you can't wander around the palace at all hours of the night as you please.

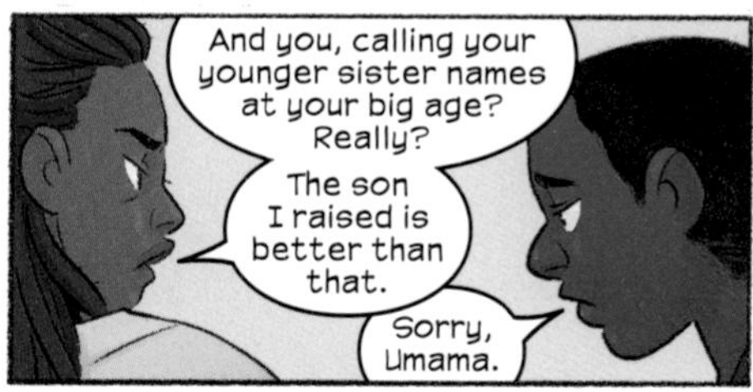
And you, calling your younger sister names at your big age? Really?
The son I raised is better than that.
Sorry, Umama.

There is an old proverb my mother used to say whenever my sister and I fought.
"A blow to your sibling's body bleeds like a blow to your own."
No matter how angry you get with each other, never forget this one thing.

The two of you are two halves of the same coin. Even if everything around you crumbles away, that never will.

Now, get to bed. We have a big day tomorrow...

"...and lots of people who are counting on us to make sure it goes well."

I can't believe it's already Soul Washing Day.

Did you see the weather this morning? Twenty percent chance of severe thunder-storms.
Do you think they'll cancel?
No way. The Soul Washing has never been canceled.
And besides, there's not a cloud in the sky!

Shuri, come let me finish your hair!

Did you put away all your tech?
Of course, Umama.
Good. We don't want to anger the ancestors by bringing anything besides the offerings to the ceremony.
And how are you feeling, nephew?
G-great!
Don't even worry about this. The Soul Washing is nothing compared to the kind of speeches you'll do when you become king.
My uncle S'Yan, current Black Panther and regent of Wakanda, former head of the Wakanda Design Group. Probably the coolest member of my family. (Behind me, of course.)

Those have millions of eyes from all over Wakanda watching your every move.
Today is only hundreds of thousands of eyes, so this is nothing!

S'Yan, stop scaring my son!
I was only trying to help!
H-h-hundreds... of...thousands...

But your uncle is right. You have nothing to fear.
You are the son of kings. Once you truly learn to believe it, no fear can sink its claws in your heart.
I won't let you down.
I know you won't. Now, let's go. It's time to begin.

My siblings, I thank you all for gathering here today to honor the ancestors of our great nation.
Our prosperity is due to their continued blessings. We walk in their steps and through their wisdom in all things.
Now we thank them for their protections and humbly request that they guide us for many years to come.
Fathers of my fathers and mothers of my mothers.
I stand before you with humble offerings on behalf of the entire River Tribe, and I bare my soul for cleansing in your healing waters.
May I return renewed with your wisdom and strength in the name of all my kinfolk.
FWOOSH

PLOP
WHOOO!

YAY!

BOOM

We should cancel the ceremony for now. It's too dangerous for people to be out on the water like this.
We can't cancel the Soul Washing. That's never been done. Perhaps we can wait for the rain to clear.

What are you doing?

I think I can help!
You know there's no tech allowed at the Soul Washing.
If someone doesn't do something soon, there won't **be** a Soul Washing!
Give it to me. You're going to get us in trouble!
Quit telling me what to do.
You're not Dad!
Shuri, give it!
Get off!

CLICK
CLICK
BZZT
BZZT
BZZT
Protect the crowd!
I've got it!
No, I've got it!
Shuri! T'Challa!
CRASH
BOOM
I've got you!

Is everyone all right? Are you hurt?
We're fine.

...Well, this is bad.

CHAPTER TWO

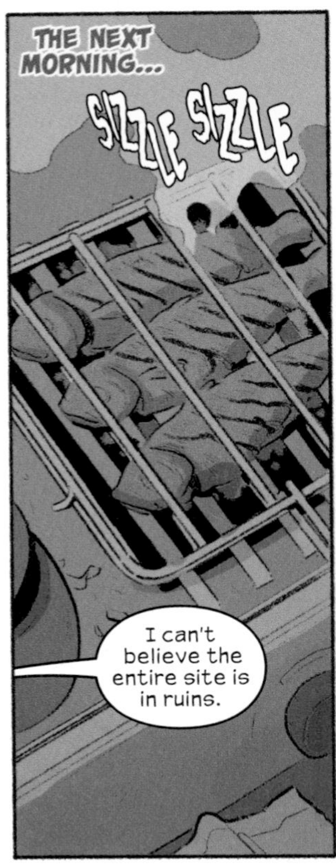
THE NEXT MORNING...
SIZZLE SIZZLE
I can't believe the entire site is in ruins.

Wakanda has never not completed the Soul Washing Ceremony before.
This is an ill omen, I tell you. The ancestors will curse us for this.

You superstitious old men need to relax. They're only children, and it was an accident.

Let's just thank Bast that no one was seriously injured and that—
GAH!
Oko!

Are you all—AH!
GAH!

I have never been more ashamed of either of you than I am at this moment.
Do you even understand the magnitude of what you've done?

What do we need to fix the site? I'll rebuild it myself—
This isn't about just the statues, young man.

The Soul Washing Ceremony was meant to be a time of humility and gratitude for all our ancestors have given us.
But because you were more concerned with your petty feud than honoring our foremothers and forefathers, you have destroyed something that can never be replaced.
To start with, your punishment will be—

—guh!
MOM!

Mom, are you okay?
GAH!
GRAAAAARH!
MOM!

My queen!

I'm sorry, Princess, but this is for your own good.
Let me go, Okoye! Mom! *Mom!*

MAMA!

They call it the techno-organic virus.

The virus works by turning organic matter into a metal-based alien tech. Once it's taken root, the hosts lose almost all semblance of control as the virus reaches into their brains.
The queen is the fifteenth case that has come in this morning alone.

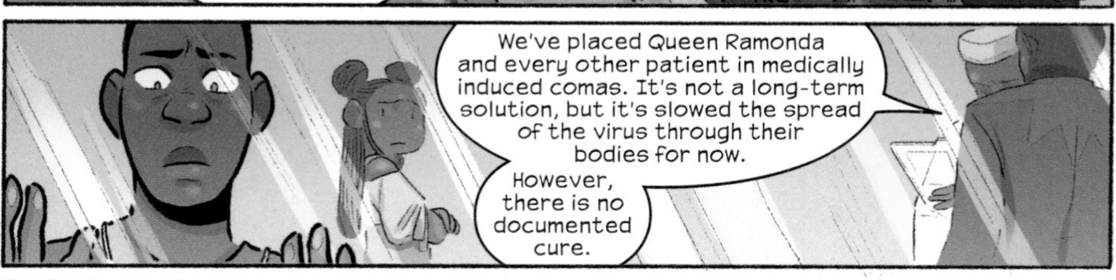
We've placed Queen Ramonda and every other patient in medically induced comas. It's not a long-term solution, but it's slowed the spread of the virus through their bodies for now.
However, there is no documented cure.

Do we know where the victims contracted the virus?
Not yet. Right now, the only thing they have in common is that all of them were present at the ceremony yesterday.

We need to start testing medicines. What trial vaccines exist? What research do we—
Shuri, Wakanda has some of the best doctors in the world. They don't need you to tell them how to do their jobs.

I think it would be better if you left.
We have many important matters to discuss.

Do you think the virus is punishment from the ancestors for what happened at the Soul Washing?
I don't want to believe it, but...
If it's true, then the princess is cursed.
CURSED

BEEP!

K'Nemi:
Are you okay?
Please call me.

Whatever's up, I've got your back. It's gonna be okay.

I am *not* cursed.
Just hang on a little longer, Mom. There's a cure to this virus...
...and I'm gonna find it.

THE PALACE LIBRARY.
If it happened in Wakanda, there's a record of it here.
One of these books has to have something about this virus.
I don't care how long it takes.
I. Am. Finding. This. Cure.
TAK TAK TAK TAK

...no matter...
...how... long...
....it...... ...takes.......

ZZZZZZZZ
SNOOORE

BAM!

Oooooooow, ow ow ow!
What's this?

Queen N'Yami was my dad's first wife. T'Challa's birth mother.
STUDIES in VIBRANIUM IRREGULARITIES
CHIEF SCIENTIST N'Yami
She died before I was born, but they say she was one of the best scientists Wakanda ever had.
Maybe there's something useful in here...

"Day 23, Log #8. Time: 10:35 a.m. Finally made headway into research on Vibranium origins and molecular structure.
"Every specimen of Vibranium tested suggests derivation from a single source...
"The Star Core.
ORIGIN: Alien
"The oldest-known piece of Vibranium in existence and the suspected source from which all the material mutated.
"Holds abilities never seen in the substance before.
"Known properties: Kinetic energy absorption and release. Enhanced durability. Ability to eradicate corrupted particles in other substances.
"Properties are consistent with oral folklore accounts of a sacred item used by ancient shamans in purging rituals.
"Tales link the Star Core to the mythic Heartlands, established in folklore as a gap between the human world and the ancestral plane.
"Storytellers claim the item was hidden so none could use it for destruction.
"However, in the right hands, the Star Core could change Wakanda for the better."
Star Core...purging abilities...
This is it!

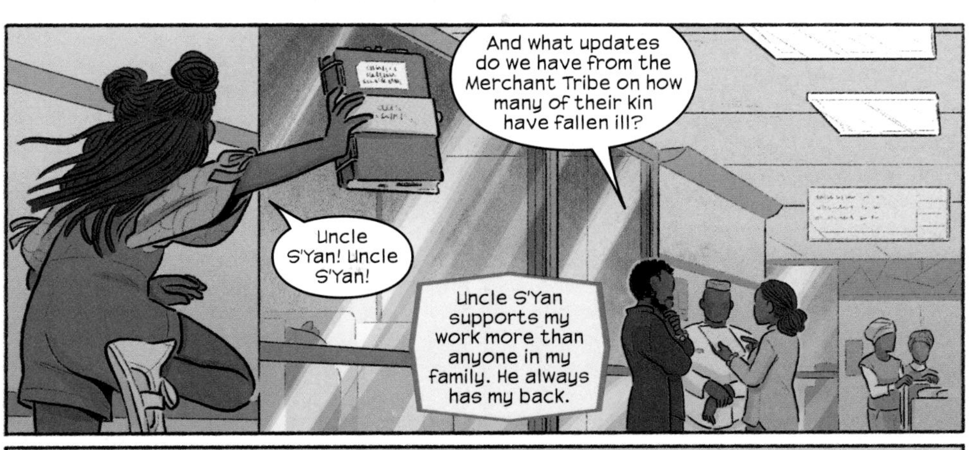
And what updates do we have from the Merchant Tribe on how many of their kin have fallen ill?
Uncle S'Yan! Uncle S'Yan!
Uncle S'Yan supports my work more than anyone in my family. He always has my back.

If anyone can help me find the Star Core, it's him.
I think I've found the answer to all our problems!
STUDIES in VIBRANIUM IRREGULARITIES
CHIEF SCIENTIST

An ancient piece of Vibranium hidden in the Heartlands?
Shuri, I don't have time to discuss children's tales right now.
It's not a children's tale!

With the Star Core, we'll be able to purge the techno-organic virus straight from the corrupted cells. We could save everybody!
No.

The Heartlands are just a myth used to scare children!
SLAM
I'm not sending my best warriors on a goose chase after a mythical item hidden in a place that doesn't exist!

But—!
I know you're worried about your mother. We all are.
Bast knows that this family can't afford to lose any more members.
STUDIES in VIBRANIUM IRREGULARITIES
CHIEF SCIENTIST N'Yami

My father... Queen N'Yami... your father...
They run like all ancestors through Djalia now. The best thing we can do to honor them is to take care of the ones they left behind.

But, Uncle—!
I will discuss this no more. You are smart, my niece. Smarter than some even twice your age.
But the difference between intelligence and wisdom is vast. A truly wise person knows when to fight...
STUDIES in VIBRANIUM IRREGULARITIES
CHIEF SCIENTIST

...and when to stay out of the way.

BEEP...
BEEP...

BEEP...
BEEP...
Just hold on a little longer, Mom.

BEEP...
BEEP...
I'm going to get you the Star Core.
Even if I have to do it all by myself.

CHAPTER THREE

The Palace of Birnin Zana is the most well-defended place in the world.
The odds of anyone busting in or out of here are highly improbable.

Like, the odds of an armadillo becoming the next Black Panther–level improbable.
KNOCK KNOCK
Princess? Would you like to play a game tonight after I have finished my rounds?
I'll even consider going easy on you on the Road of the Rainbow.
SHURI'S ROOM
Keep out
(that means you, T'CHALLA!)

No thank you. I'm good!
And for the millionth time, it's Rainbow Road.

Are you sure? After everything that's happened, I thought... you shouldn't be alone right now.
I'm good, really!
...If you insist.

Good night, my princess.
Good night!
BZZT
Luckily, the gap between improbable and impossible is where I do my best work.

Have I already mentioned what a bad idea this is?
Only about a thousand times.
Here's a thousand and one: This is a bad idea.
Did Okoye buy the hologram?

Yep. And you have about ten minutes until the video I looped over the live security footage cuts out, so make them count.
Guards on your two o'clock!

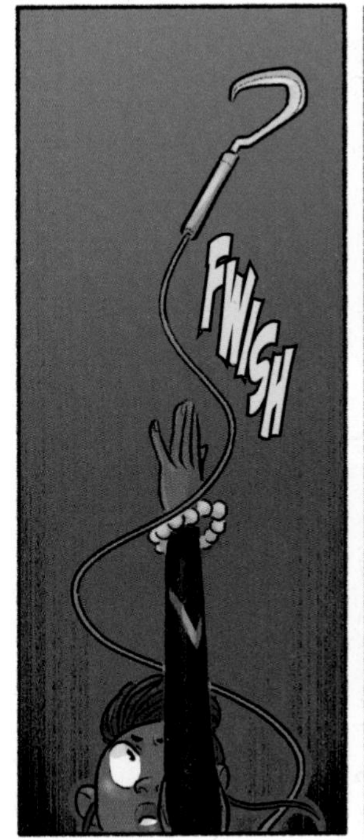
FWISH

Six minutes till the transport leaves.
Got it!

The coordinates Queen N'Yami left behind are located deep in the heart of Mount Bashenga.
And every evening at nine o'clock on the dot, a transport leaves from the palace with supplies for the Wakanda Design Group headquarters located in—you guessed it!
Mount Bashenga.
If I can just make this flight, I'll be good to go.

So far so—
Where do you think you're going?

How did you know where to find me?
Uncle S'Yan mentioned you yelling something about the Heartlands, and Okoye mentioned you turned down a chance to play *Mario Kart*, which you never do.
Putting two and two together was easy from there.

Go back to your room.
If you would just let me explain!

Haven't you caused enough trouble already?
Ugh, you never listen to me!
BEEP

Ah!
SLAM!

WHIIIIIIR

FWOOSH

Hey! There's been a mistake! Let us out!
Don't waste your breath. There's no way the pilot can hear you.
BANG BANG

As soon as we land, we're getting on the next ship home.
If you could just stop yelling for five seconds and let me explain!
I was doing some research, and I think I've found a cure for the techno-organic virus.

It's called the Star Core. It's the oldest piece of Vibranium in the world, and in ancient times, they used it to purge impurities from other substances.
It's supposed to be hidden somewhere in the Heartlands. If we find it, we can use it to save everyone.

Uh-huh. And exactly who is this absurd person who thinks something so powerful was hidden in a fantasy land?

Your mother.

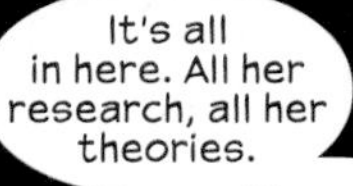

It's all in here. All her research, all her theories.
I know it sounds ridiculous, but Queen N'Yami believed the Star Core and the Heartlands were both real.

You were too young to help when your birth mother passed.
There was nothing you or anyone else could have done.

But this time, you're not powerless. This time, you can help.
STUDIES in VIBRANIUM IRREGULARITIES
HIEF SCIENTIST
N'Yami

How could we even live with ourselves if this virus kills Mom, and we didn't try everything we possibly could to save her?
One. Hour.
You have one hour to find a way into the Heartlands once we land.
If you can't, we go back, and you'll drop this Star Core talk for good.

One hour.
I can work with that.
Mount Bashenga. Home of the Wakanda Design Group and the only known Vibranium mound in the world.

POP!

I think I just saw the prince and princess!
Not now, M'Baku.
But—!

How are the cameras looking, K'Nemi?
BZZT
They're handled but— breaking—up— only—few minutes—
BZZT

There it is! The coordinates say the entrance to the Heartlands is right up—

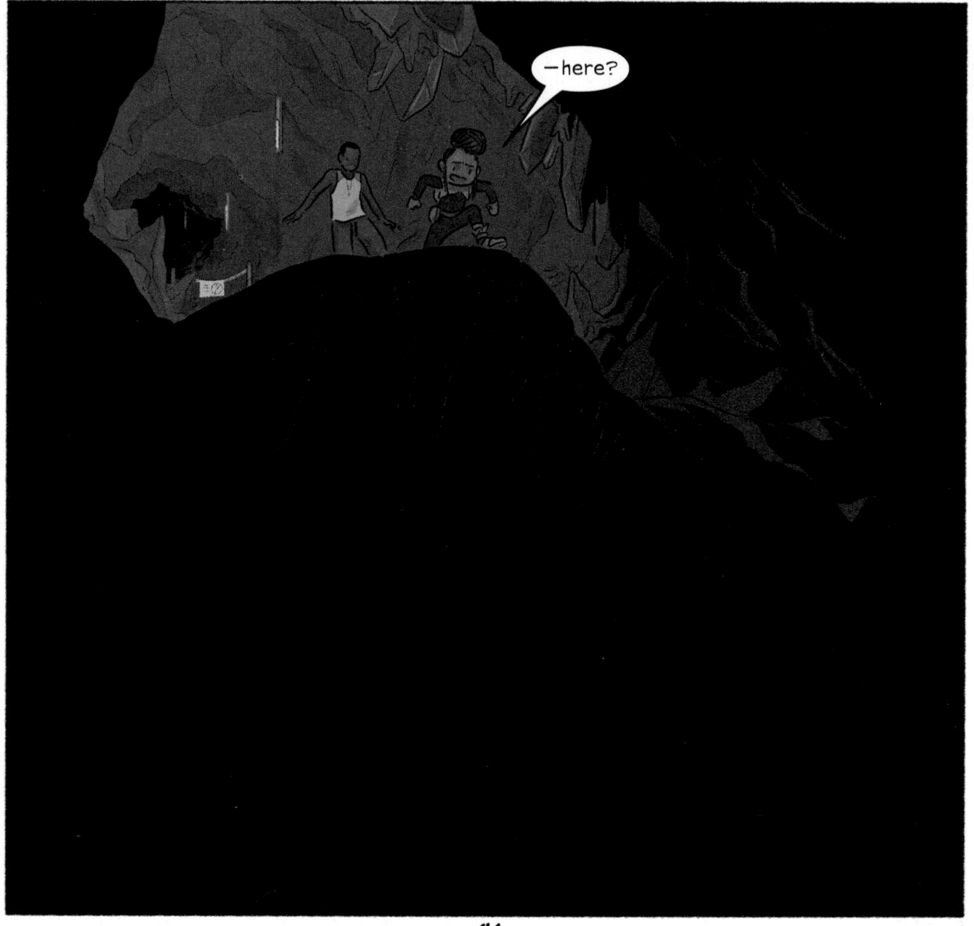
—here?

I—I don't understand. It's supposed to be right here! Why isn't it here?

Maybe we need to go down—
Are you out of your mind?
I've indulged this long enough. It's time to go.

NO! I'M NOT GOING TO GO BACK AND WATCH MOM DIE!

I think they went this way!

PRINCE T'CHALLA! PRINCESS SHURI!

CHAPTER FOUR

Log #42.
Time:
...Unknown.
Location:
...Somewhere.

This must be the Heartlands...T'Challa, we made it!

...T'Challa?

T'Challa!

Yes, Prime Minister... I would love the key...to Chocolate World...

Get up.
GAH!

Wh-where are we?
Where else, dummy?
The Heartlands, of course!

But this doesn't make any sense. How did we—
Who cares how it happened—we made it!
There's no signal, though. Guess the Heartlands isn't part of our usual service area.
The coordinates in the journal ended at the mine, but the Temple of the Star Core is supposed to be deep in the center of the Heartlands.
I don't think swimming back into the ocean is going to help us.
So I guess we gotta go that way.
Shuri, if we're really doing this, you have to **promise** me you won't do anything stupid or reckless.
That means no going off on your own and no doing whatever you want without consulting me first.
Yeah, yeah, no running off, no talking to strangers.
Can we please get going?
Let's go.

Stay close. Don't touch anything.
This is amazing. It's just like all the stories used to say.
The stories also mentioned child-eating giants, which is why you need to stay close.
Just come on!

Hang on, we are ***definitely*** going in circles!
Still no sign of the temple...
No way. We've been walking in a straight line.
Didn't we just pass this place?

Let me lead. You clearly don't know where you're going.
And you do?

Would it kill you to admit just once that maybe there's something I could do that you can't?
Right, like getting us lost in the middle of Bast knows where?

Perhaps I may be of some assistance?
AH!

TALKING RAT! TALKING RAT!
Talking rat?!
Excuse you, for I am clearly a jerboa.
Pah, "talking rat"... rats and jerboas are completely different families of Rodentia!

Do we...do we have jerboas in Wakanda?
Are we even *in* Wakanda?
Look at your elders when they're speaking to you!

You say you're from Wakanda?
If that's the case, you'll need a guide through the mystical labyrinth that is the Heartlands, and you'll find none better than me.

All I ask is that you take me back to Wakanda when you—
Gah!
We appreciate your offer, but no thank you. Goodbye.

The impertinence! The disrespect! Never in all my years—is this how the youth of Wakanda are raised nowadays?!
Come on, Shuri!

Do you know where the Temple of the Star Core is?
Yes, I do. I'd be happy to take you there.
T'Challa, do you hear that? He knows how to get to the temple!

No way. We have no idea what that creature is, or if we can even trust him.
I wouldn't go that way if I were you.

Thank you for your concern, but I—
Gah!
T'Challa!

WHAM!
See what happens when you don't listen to your elders?

GRRRRRR
I am so, so sorry. I didn't mean to intrude!

Ah!
Hey! Let him go!

CHOMP
GRAAAAAAAWR
WHAM
WHAM
WHAM
WHAM

Do you still believe you don't need my help?

Who are you, truly?
I... I don't know.
Centuries ago, I woke up in the Heartlands trapped in this form with no memories.
I couldn't even remember my own name.

All I know for sure is that Wakanda was a place of great importance to me, and that I was once human just like you.

I've tried to go back, but I've never been able to cross the boundary between worlds on my own. That's why I need your help.
Please, take me with you when you return to Wakanda. Take me home.

Aw, come on, T'Challa...
How can you say no to that face?

Pleaaaaaaaaase.
Ughhhhhhh.

Okay, fine, he can come!
YIPPEE!

What should we call you until we find your true name?
Call me whatever you wish.
But make sure you choose something honorable.

A powerful moniker that a distinguished warrior may wear into battle with pride.
Hmmmm...

I'm gonna call you Mustard!
What?!
Nice to meet you, Mustard!

CHAPTER FIVE

THE BOG OF LOST DREAMS.
Legend says you can't trust anything you see in this part of the Heartlands.
But Mustard says if we want to reach the temple, we've gotta cross this first.
...And then everything blew up, and the next day, people all over the city started getting sick!
That's why we need the Star Core.
Fascinating! A device that can change the weather...Vibranium has come far indeed since Wakanda first began.
Are you two going to start helping, or am I supposed to row us out of the world's creepiest swamp all by myself?

I built us a boat. What more do you want?
But back to the whole "you used to be human" thing, because I have some questions.
One: What did you do to get someone angry enough to turn you into a jerboa?
Two: Why a jerboa and not something cool, like, I don't know, a wolverine? And why do you speak like a grandpa?
If I could answer those questions, I wouldn't need your help at all.

Maybe you were a criminal, and your transformation is your punishment.
Criminal?! Would a common criminal have such a strong moral code or miss the feeling of using a spear to defend our homeland this much?
I may not know who I am, but it's not a criminal. Who are yo to be making such accusations, anyway?

You are in the presence of Prince T'Challa and Princess Shuri, current heirs to the throne of Wakanda.
You're next in line for the throne?

You, the future king of Wakanda!
I don't see what's so funny about it.
The king of Wakanda is meant to be a pillar of unity, the only one who protects the people. Do you have what it takes to be that kind of leader?

The Dora Milaje do just as much work to protect the people as the king does.
I don't know what that is. Besides, what kind of king unleashes a curse on his own people?

I don't think the virus is a curse at all!
I've been thinking about it, and something doesn't add up.
How come only people who were at the Soul Washing have gotten sick?

I think they were targeted. T'Challa, what do you think?
...Yeah, that could be it...

Huh?
T'Challaaaaaaaa
T'Challaaaaaaa
Where are you going?
I'm just...
T'Challa, wait!
F-Father... and...Mother?
Of course it's me, my son! We've been looking everywhere for you!

It's been so long.
It really has.
Have you been keeping up with my brother's training?
Yes, I have!
Of course you have. I'd expect nothing less from my baby boy.
Oh, did I tell you about the newest break-through in my research?
No, tell me everything!
T'Challa?

Is this your deepest desire?
A world where I was never born?
I—

That's what this is!
In a world where Queen N'Yami lived, our dad and my mom never would have met.
They never would have had me.

Is that why you're always upset with me? Because deep down, you wish I'd never been born?

I...

Shuri, wait!

Stupid T'Challa.
Stupid, never-ending nightmare bog.
SLAM
You don't need T'Challa.

You don't need anyone but yourself.
T'Challa, Uncle S'Yan, even our mother...they're all holding you back.
Holding *us* back.
You are capable of extraordinary things. And that terrifies them.
You don't need them. You never have.
Stay here with me—
—and become the Black Panther and queen you were always meant to be.

Me...Black Panther and queen...
Stay here and you'll be second to none. No one will push you to the side or order you around ever again.
All you have to do is stay.
All I have to do is...
Wait...
Where's *my* mom?
This isn't real. You're not real. I have to find the Star Core so I can go home.
My *real* home.
This *is* your home! *I'm* all you need!
Get off me!

Stay with me, Shuri.
I can make you a queen, Shuri.
Let me go!
Go back to what, always being second best?
Forever living in the shadow of a brother who never wanted you?
STAY STAY STAY STAY STAY STAY STAY STAY STAY
Up here, you overgrown weed!

Let go of my sister!
GWAAAAH!!
THWACK

All right, time to go!

STAY
STAY
STAY
STAY
STAY

BWOOSH
We should be safe now. Its power can't extend past the bog.

Are you all right? Did you get hurt anywhere?
I'm fine.
...About what you saw earlier—

Forget it. We need to keep moving.

There's nothing more to say.

The sooner we get out of here, the better.

BOOM
Ugh, how much longer until—
We're here.

Welcome to the Temple of the Star Core.
Are there any traps?
Not that I'm aware of, but tread with care.

Something about this place weirds me out.

Mustard, how far are we from the core?

What the—
It's just up ahead!
Shuri, it's *here!*
Take care, little ones.
This water contains all the emotions of every person who has ever called Wakanda home.
Fall in there, and the weight of it all will keep you down forever.
Whoa, it's even brighter in person...
Got it!

Huh, no traps. You'd think something this important would have at least one trap protecting it.
Are you complaining because we're not being attacked?
Relax, bro, we did it! Thank you so much, Mustard!
A true warrior keeps his promises, and I promised I'd bring you here.

Hang on, Mom.
We're coming.
Is something the matter?

Nothing, it's just...
I've been thinking a lot about what your real name could be, and I've got a theory.
You don't remember any specific details of who you used to be, but you're an expert on Wakandan politics.
Plus you mentioned how much you miss fighting with a spear.

And earlier, your shadow didn't look like a jerboa...
...it looked like a panther.

I think when you were human, you were the Black Panther. And not just any Black Panther.

I think you were Bashenga, the very first king of Wakanda.

My name is... Bashenga?
Yes... Yes...
My name *is* Bashenga!
What's happening?!
I don't know!
WOOOOOOOSH
"Like all those in my generation, I came of age among war and bloodshed.
"When the war to unite the tribes of Wakanda finally came to an end, all I wanted was to make the peace last.
"Nkosenye was the leader of the Hyena Clan, my second-in-command during the war, and a brother to me in all but blood."
We could not have achieved this victory without you, dear friend.
When the Hyena and Panther Clans work together, no force on this earth can stop us.
"But though the war was won, the work was not yet finished. Now was the time to pick the leader who would guide Wakanda forward.
"Wakanda needed a king, and I could think of no better choice than myself.

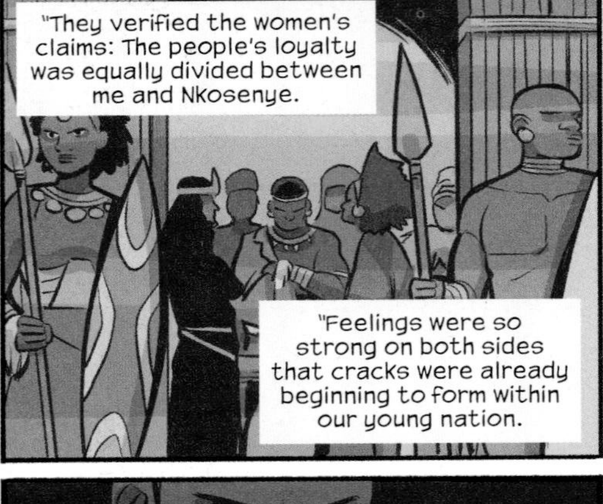

"Something had to be done.

"Though Hyena Clan was one of the first groups to join the new Wakanda, they kept loyal to the war god Wepwawet over our panther goddess Bast.
"There were many who distrusted Wepwawet's followers and wanted them out of the alliance."

What is the meaning of this? Unhand me!
Waaa, Mama! Help!

Bashenga, my brother, please help. There's been some kind of misunderstanding...
Today, I learned of a devastating plot by the Hyena Clan to force us all into worship of their war god.
That is why, with a heavy heart, I order them to leave so we can secure our hard-won peace.

"It may seem harsh, but I did what I had to do for Wakanda.
ALL HAIL KING BASHENGA!
ALL HAIL KING BASHENGA!
"It was the only way...

"All...hail...King... Bashenga..."
You... you...
How could you?!
You exiled an innocent man and his people so you could have the throne all to yourself!
A battle for the throne would have spilled innocent blood we could not afford to lose.
I did what I had to do to maintain peace.
That's why the ancestors turned you into a jerboa after your death, to punish you for what you did!
Did my choice not pave the way for Wakanda to thrive the way it has?
Did my decision not lead us to become the most advanced nation in the world?
Is it not because of me that you two were even *born?*
As soon as we return home, we're telling everyone what really happened to the Hyena Clan.

Do you realize... that could lead to our family's banishment?!
And if that's the case... fine.
The people deserve to know the truth of your crimes.
But... my legacy... Everything I worked for... You can't...
No.

NO!
FWOOSH

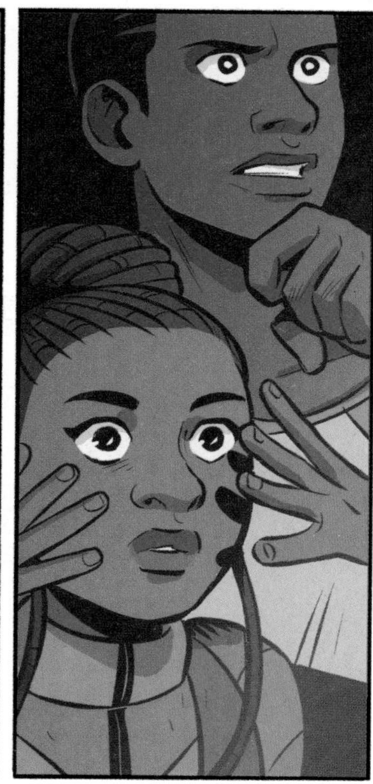

GRRRRRR
After all I did to secure Wakanda's future...no one shall threaten it.
Not even you, Prince.
T'CHALLA!

CHAPTER SIX

SWISH

Come on!
Wait, the Star Core!
The Star Core can't help anyone if that thing rips our faces off!
I don't wish to fight you, children. Since we are family, I'll offer you a deal.

Vow that you'll tell no one of what you learned here, and I'll return the Star Core to you.
T'Challa... maybe we should take the deal.

Without the core, the techno-organic virus will kill everyone. It'll kill Mom! We can't leave without it!
I know! I know...but lying to our people for the rest of our lives about what our ancestor did?

I—I can't do that.
I can't be that kind of king.
I *won't* be that kind of king.

Hey, about what you saw back in the Bog of Lost Dreams.
Does that really matter right now?
!?

It matters to me.
Everything I know about my birth mother, I learned second-hand.

She brought me into this world, and all I have to remember her by is other people's stories of what she was like.
Grieving someone you've never known...it's like being born with a hole in your heart.
Some days it's easier to ignore than other days, but you never forget that it's there.

So yeah, sometimes I wonder what my life would have been like if she'd—if she'd lived.

If they'd *both* lived.

But that never, *ever* meant I wish you hadn't been born.
I know that big science brain of yours doesn't like contradictions, but it's true.
I wish my birth mom hadn't died, but I wouldn't change having you for a sister for anything.

I love you, little sis.
Even if you do drive me absolutely bonkers.

When you see an opening, grab the Star Core and run for the exit as fast as you can.
No matter what happens to me, make sure you and the core get home.
What are you—?

Over here, grandpa!
T'CHALLA!

Who cares about the Star Core? I'm getting out of here, and as soon as I do, I'm going to tell everyone what you did.
No!

GROOOOOOOOOOW!

ROAAAAR!

SLAM

SPLASH

T'CHALLA!

T'CHALLA!

T'Challa, he's—
H-he can't be—
He's not—

I've got to get out of here.
I have to get back to Wakanda.

I have to save Mom.
I have to save everyone.
I have to—

Stand, Shuri.
Huh?
Q-Queen N'Yami?
How is this possible?
The Heartlands are a place born of power and memory. You were in need, so I came.
Like Mustard...

I don't deserve your kindness.
Not when I was only born because you died! Not when I'm the reason your son is d-d-...gone.
Life is not lived in "if"s, Shuri.
Do not waste it torturing yourself over things that could not be.
Save that energy for the people who need you most.
Me? But I can't fight off an entire lake. I'm not strong enough.
On the contrary, you're the only one who can.
After all...

...you're two halves of the same coin.

SNIFF

Come out, little princess.
Promise to keep my secret, and I will save your brother and take you home.

PING!

Hm?
SPLASH

...unworthy...
...failure prince...
...embarrassment...
...utter disgrace...

Gah!
I don't deserve to go back. I don't deserve to be prince of Wakanda. I shouldn't even be the prince...

Forget about me...I'm no one important...

You're not a failure! You're not a disappointment!
You're the son of N'Yami and T'Chaka and Ramonda! Nephew of S'Yan! Prince and future king of Wakanda!
You're also a complete pain in the butt who wouldn't know the word "fun" if it was literally tattooed on your forehead!
You care more about people than anyone I've ever met, and you're the hardest-working person I know!
You are my brother, and you... are...coming... with...me!
CRACK

FWOOSH

SPLASH
COUGH
COUGH

...You okay?
Yeah, you?
Been better, but I'll live.

There you are, children.

Now, back to our conversation...

You fell into the lake. You saw everything the role of king demands of a person.
Dredging up the tale of the Hyena Clan will jeopardize our hard-won safety.

Do you really wish to be the ones who threaten thousands of years of peace?

Yes.
We do.

What—!
You're the one who doesn't understand what Wakanda needs right now, not us.
"When we were little, our father always told us tales of the kings of old.
"How we should live up to the legacy they left behind by being just and fair to our people..."
...All of our people.
So even if you are our ancestor, we can't keep this charade going for you.
I don't care what you thought at the time. Exiling Hyena Clan was wrong.
If this comes out, it could mean chaos. Another war.
You would jeopardize your own reign before it even begins?
If that's what the people choose, then fine.
I don't want to be king if it means being a liar.

Oh, Bast...
What have I done?

RUMBLE
What in the name of Bast—
I think the ancestors want us to get out of here!
Is this part of the Soul Washing Ceremony curse?
There is no curse...
...But I sense the answers you seek on the Soul Washing can be found by looking into the past.
Wait, what do you mean there's no curse?
If there's no curse, then where did the virus come from...
Unless it was...man-made... That's it!

Run!
CRASH

BOOM

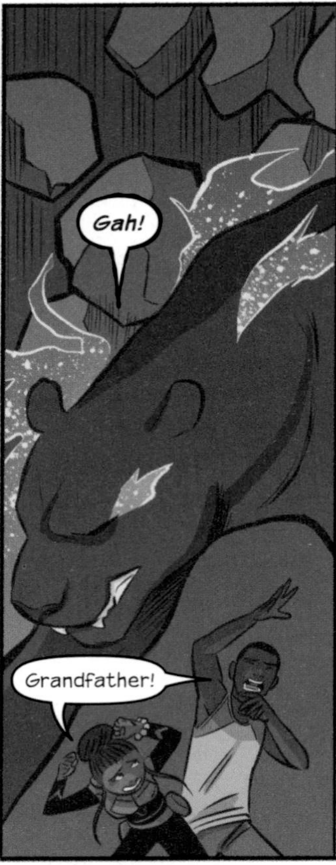
Gah!
Grandfather!

Leave this place, now. The water will take you home, same as it brought you here.
But what about you?
Do not worry about me—you cannot kill one who has already passed.

My time in Wakanda has come to an end.
It is time that I move on to the next stage of my existence, watching over you all instead of dictating your choices.
And hopefully someday, the ancestors will welcome me back into Djalia with open arms.

And it is time for the truth about Hyena Clan to come out.
The *whole* truth.

Hamba kakuhle, Grandfather.
Hambani kakuhle, children.
May your lives be long and full of light.

CRASH

There it is!
Together now.
One.
Two.
THREE!

CHAPTER SEVEN

Come on, K'Nemi, think.
There has to be some way to stabilize this antidote even without the Star Core.

You're certainly here late.

S-Shuri! You're back!
Yep, just arrived. I know you were worried, so I came straight here.
I have the Star Core, too.

Hang on, there's no way to know if that thing will actually stop the curse. Let me take a look at it—
I know you're the one who spread the virus.

What are you talking about? You sure you didn't hit your head out there?
That streak in your hair.
It's the exact same as Nkosenye's.
Same as his necklace.
You're his descendant. A member of the Hyena Clan.
And you've been using the resources here at the WDG to develop the techno-organic virus.
I'm honestly surprised you didn't figure it out sooner.

Why are you doing this?
If you learned the truth about what happened to Nkosenye, then you understand why I had to avenge him.
Innocent people have been hurt!

Innocent people were hurt when your ancestor exiled my entire clan for no reason!

"Hyena Clan causes misfortune wherever they go."
"They're just a bunch of scavengers and thieves who deserve their exile."
"I've lived my whole life under the weight of these prejudices over something my people didn't even do.

"I've managed to pass in Wakandan society by never being open about my heritage.
"But I knew I couldn't stand by during the Soul Washing and watch your family spread lies about Wakanda's founding.
"Someone needed to pay for what happened to Nkosenye, and every Hyena Clan member since him."

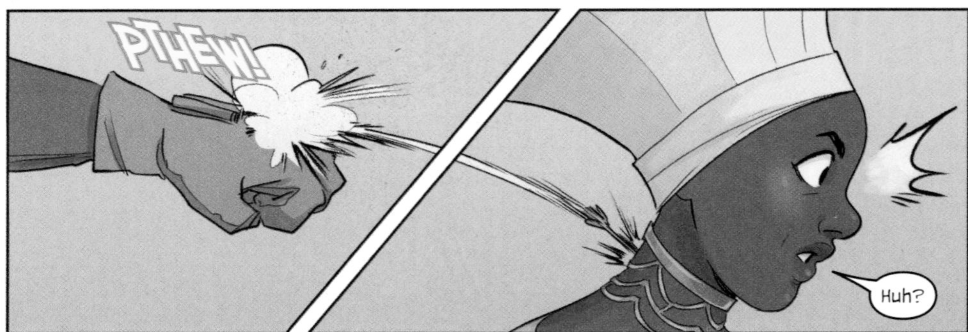
PTHEW!
Huh?

I didn't plan on you and your brother destroying the ceremony site. But it heightened people's belief that you and by extension Panther Tribe were cursed.
Then I could come in with the antidote to fix the crisis, no fairy-tale magic Star Core needed.
That would prove that your family aren't the perfect saviors you pretend to be.

You're right.

What?
I said you're right. What Bashenga did to Hyena Clan was wrong and needs to be made right.
We can make it right—together.

Stop all this virus mess, and let's work together like we used to.

As if a member of my family would trust a promise from yours ever again.

PTHEW!
THUNK

WHIIIRR... CLICK
CLICK CLICK

K'NEMI!

That should keep her occupied for a little—

Oof!

Give it up, K'Nemi. We heard everything.

K'Nemi, please. We can still work this out.

Take one more step toward me, and I will break your precious Star Core.
You'll never cure your mother without it.

I'm not so sure about that.
Why don't you open the box and see for yourself?

CLICK
HI!

Ah!

PFFFFFFFFFT...

How did you—
I lied earlier. T'Challa and I actually returned to Wakanda several hours ago.

"The magic of the Heartlands brought us back to Mount Bashenga, the same as we entered."

AHHHHHHH!

"My uncle was about as mad as you'd expect that we'd been missing for days when we finally got back to Birnin Zana.
"Honestly, madder, probably.

"However, he calmed down a bit when he saw what we brought.
"I'm still grounded, like, forever, though.

"The real Star Core is back at the palace infirmary.
"They're using it to cure our mom and all the other victims of your attack right now.
"After we gave up the Star Core, I had some time to think about everything— the virus, our ancestors, the nature of the attack."

I realized you were the only one who had enough reason and know-how to pull something like this off.
That's when we set up this trap. I wasn't sure you'd fall for the fake Star Core gambit.
"But you did.
"After all, we were friends."

Why wouldn't friends trust each other?

So you've caught me. What happens now? You'll throw me in prison or exile me just like my ancestors?
No.

I'll never agree with what you did...but I get why you did it.
Which is why I think rather than just locking you away, a more just punishment would be to help fix what was broken.
I meant what I said about us working together.

There is a better future for Wakanda.
One we can make.

Wha—
CRASH
Are you okay?
I'm fine.
Message the city guard that the culprit has escaped. I want everyone on high alert!

Now we need to—
Prince T'Challa! Princess Shuri!

It's your mother!

We didn't think you were—
—it was all **SHURI**, she's the one who saved you—
—no, without T'Challa I wouldn't have been able to—

I know.
I know, I know, I know.

What happened with the young Hyena?
She got away, but the Dora are on it.
Would you like to go after her?

No, the Dora can handle that. There's something else T'Challa and I need to do first.
What is it, my dear?

"Something that should have been done a long time ago."
2 WEEKS LATER.

Whoa, there are way more people than I expected. You gonna be okay?
Y—yeah.

H-hello everybody... t-thank you for...
....T-thank you for—

Several days ago, we gathered here to give thanks to our ancestors.
We assumed that every tribe was represented at the time. But they were not.
Hyena Clan was excluded, as they have been from both Wakanda's present and past.
Not of their own choice as we've been taught to believe, but because my ancestor Bashenga forced them out.

What he did hurt people—our people. Just as we acknowledge our ancestors' achievements, so too must we acknowledge their mistakes.

On behalf of the entire Panther Tribe, I apologize and vow that we will spend the rest of our lives trying to repair what he broke.
Starting today, by restoring the statue of Nkosenye, the Hyena Clan ancestor, to its rightful place.

You know, I still stand by what I said earlier.
All the best things *do* happen at night.
You can't see fireworks during the day, after all.

Or fireflies.
Or stars.

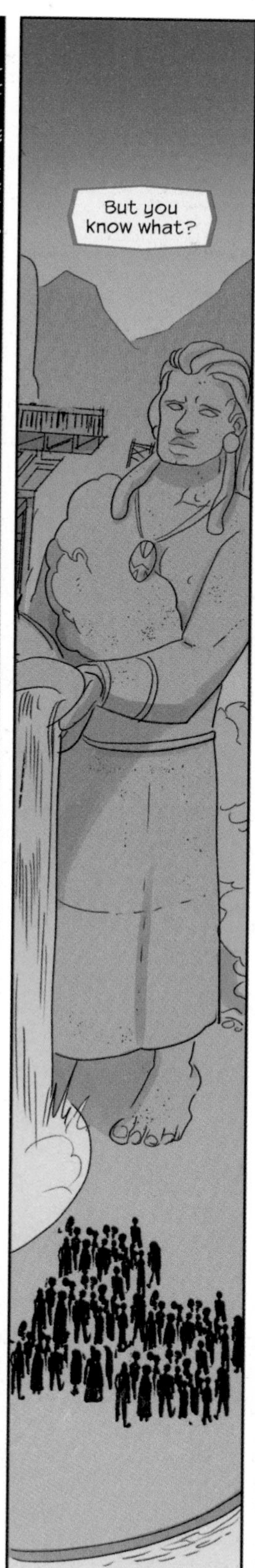
But you know what?

The days are starting to look pretty good, too.

ROSEANNE A. BROWN was born in Kumasi, Ghana, and immigrated to the wild jungles of central Maryland as a child. She graduated from the University of Maryland with a bachelor's degree in journalism and was also a teaching assistant for the school's Jiménez-Porter Writers' House program. Her debut novel, *A Song of Wraiths and Ruin*, was an instant *New York Times* bestseller, a BuzzFeed Best YA Book of the Year, and a *Boston Globe* Best Book of the Year, among other accolades. Her middle-grade debut, *Serwa Boateng's Guide to Vampire Hunting*, will be out in Fall 2022 with Rick Riordan Presents.

DIKA ARAÚJO is a Brazilian comic artist and freelance illustrator based in Sâo Paulo. Her comic book work has appeared in several Brazilian indie anthologies, one of which (*Amor em Quadrinhos*) was nominated for an Angoulême International Comics Award in 2018. She has also worked as a character and prop designer, as well as a concept artist for Brazilian animated series, such as *Oswaldo* (Cartoon Network) and *Anittinha's Club* (Gloob).

NATACHA BUSTOS is a Spanish comic book artist who drew the story "Going Nowhere," written by Brandan Montclare, for DC/Vertigo's *Strange Sports Stories*. Bustos then made her Marvel Comics debut on Spider-Woman before reteaming with Montclare and cowriter Amy Reeder on the inaugural run of *Moon Girl and Devil Dinosaur*, winner of a Glyph Award for Best Female Character in 2016. In 2020, she drew the *Buffy the Vampire Slayer: Willow* miniseries (BOOM! Studios) and became part of Marvel's Stormbreakers artist program, dedicated to spotlighting the next generation of elite artists.

CLAUDIA AGUIRRE is a Mexican, Lesbian comic book artist and writer, cofounder of Boudika Comics, GLAAD Award Nominee, and Will Eisner Award nominee. Her comic works include: Marvel's *Voices*, *Lost on Planet Earth* (ComiXology Originals), *Hotel Dare* (BOOM! Studios), *Firebrand* (Legendary Comics), *Morning in America* (OniPress), and *Kim&Kim* (Black Mask Studios).

CHECK OUT A SNEAK PEEK OF

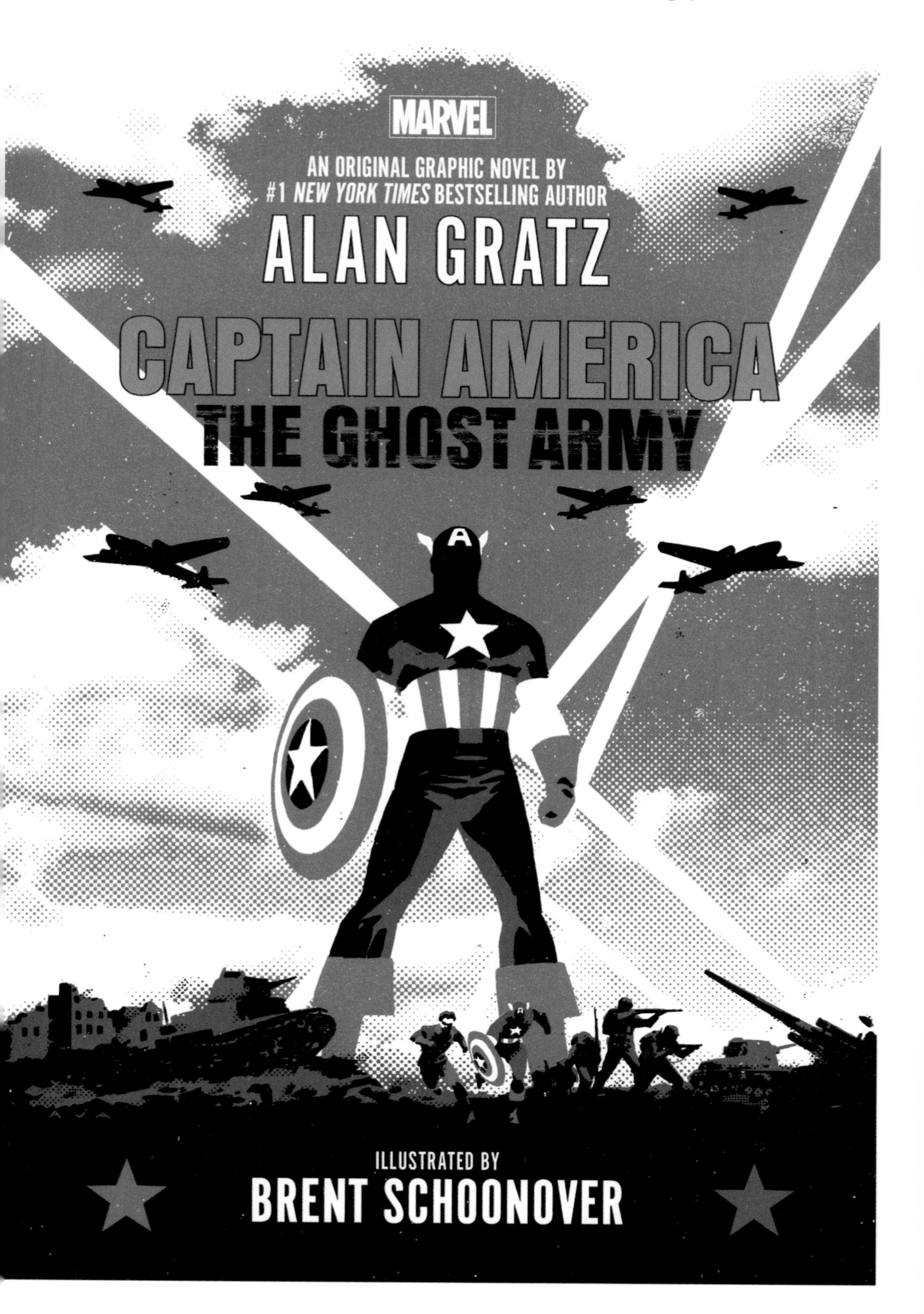

Transsia. World War II.
The eastern front.
TING
TING
TIN
TING
PO

THWACK
Gah!

Cap, we're outnumbered and outgunned!

KOW PAKOW
RAT-TAT-TAT-TAT
POOM
CRACK

Our orders are to help this British unit hold their position, Bucky, so we hold!
TINK
CRUNCH

KA-BOOM
K-CLANK K-CLANK
CRUNCH
You might want to tell that to the German panzer that just showed up!

THOOM!
KABOOM!

KRANG
Hey, Cap, check out the fancy neckwear on this guy!

Sterb, Amerikaner!

RAT-TAT-TAT-TAT
FWIP
FWIP
FWIP
FWIP

THOCK

Thanks. I owe you one.
Yeah you do! Name's Dugan. "Dum Dum" to my friends.

Well, Dum Dum, it looks like we're not gonna be around long enough to hear the story behind that nickname.
Somebody get on the radio! See if the Allies can send reinforcements!

No ground units anywhere nearby! No air support, either!

This would be a great time for that save you owe me!
I'm running out of ideas here. Buck, you got anything?

K-CLANK
K-CLANK
VROOOM
CRUNCH
What now?

K-CLANK K-CLANK
CRUNCH K-CRUNCH
VROOOM
Second Infantry, attack! Armored divisions, flank them on the west!

THUMP THUMP THUMP THUMP
THUMP THUMP
THUMP THUMP
CH-CHAK CH-CHAK CH-CHAK

Sounds like the cavalry is coming!

Looks like the Germans think so, too!

TROMP TROMP TROMP
We're saved!

CLANK CLANK CLANK
I don't get it. They told us there weren't any reinforcements nearby.

CLANK TROMP CRUNCH
From the sound of it, it's gotta be the whole Seventh Army!
Here they come!